heirloom holiday toy

jingle bells

mittens

peppermint bark

star tree topper

jumping gingerbread

eggnog

tiny penguin candle

holiday card

snorkeling elf

old-fashioned ornaments

Lump of coal

fancy present

snickerdoodle

juggling snowman

reindeer stocking

advent calendar

holly berries

A CHRISTMAS TOO BIG

by Colleen Madden

two lions

FA LA LAAAA!
Jingle jingle Jingle jingle
Bumpity Bumpity Bumpity Bumpity
WOOO—YEah!

The day after THANKSGIVING, my family goes TOTALLY BERSERK with Christmas.

My dad becomes a MINI-LIGHT STRING MASTER.
We don't need to replace these twinkle bulbs, Kerry.

While my mom turns into an . . .

ALL-CHRISTMAS . . .

ALL-THE-TIME . . .

. . . music machine!

We watch every. Single. Christmas. Special.

On every. Single. Christmas. Channel.

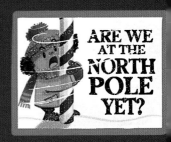

My little brother hides them all around the house.
Then hides them again.

And **again**!

AND **AGAIN!**

The week before Christmas, we bring home our tree . . .

. . . and decorate it.
Maybe just trim a BIT off the top?
Wow!
EPIC.
O.M. Gingerbread.
fa la la la

IT'S THE BIGGEST CHRISTMAS TREE EVER.

How in PEPPERMINT COCOA
are we going to hang ornaments on that thing?

It seems that everybody is having a **CHRISTMAS TOO BIG**.

Except maybe my neighbor, Mrs. Flores.

I help with the cart, and Mrs. Flores thanks me in Spanish.

Mrs. Flores asks if I'd like cocoa.

Mrs. Flores has a nice house.

I look around while she calls my mom
to let her know I'm here.

Mrs. Flores has a funny cat called Popcorn. *Palomitas de maíz* in Spanish!

Pal for short.

Her Christmas tree is trimmed with tiny paper flowers.
And that's it.

No singing penguins or peppermint candy canes . . .

. . . or a zillion lights.

I ask about the picture by her tree.

She tells me that they are in another country.

I think they must miss her too.

Then Mrs. Flores shows me how to make her beautiful flowers . . .
one color after the other.

While we work, she sings a song from when she was a girl.

En invierno,
Las flores no crecen,
esperan a que lleguen la
primavera y el sol!

In winter, the flowers
aren't blooming.
They wait for the spring
and the sun!

ELLas desean besos
cálidos de mariposa,

They wish for warm
butterfly kisses,

Luego eLLas baiLan!

then they dance!

¡Sí! ¡Sí! ¡Sí!
Yes! Yes! Yes!
La! La! La!

Mrs. Flores and I **dance** and **sing** like butterfly snowflakes.

We decorate the house with our flowers . . .

. . . and light a **special candle**.

Para mi familia.

Mrs. Flores received a Christmas gift from her family.

We open it.

She doesn't know how to use it.

But I do.

It was time for me to head home.

What a different kind of Christmas.

Small and quiet, yet **BIG** all the same.

Maybe I could find a way to have my **OWN** kind
of Christmas in my own crazy Christmas house.

Mom helps me light a candle.

This is for Mrs. Flores and her family.

Let's invite Mrs. Flores over for Christmas dinner.

How to Make Flores de Navidad!

You will need:

- 6 or more sheets of tissue paper
- A pipe cleaner, skinny "flower wire," or small rubber band • Scissors

1 Take 3 colors—6 sheets apiece. Trim to 3 sizes like this:

2 Fold all pieces like an accordion, back and forth, back and forth. Like this:

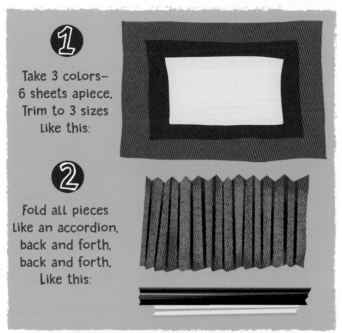

You can make cool petals by trimming the edges like this:

pipe cleaner
4–5 inches long

3

4 Take the pipe cleaner, flower wire, or rubber band and wrap it around the middle of all 3 like this:

5 Now slowly open up your flower on each side by gently pulling and scrunching the petals up toward the middle like this:

Open up and fan out the layers.

Crunch and push them up toward the middle.

Poof them up with your fingers.

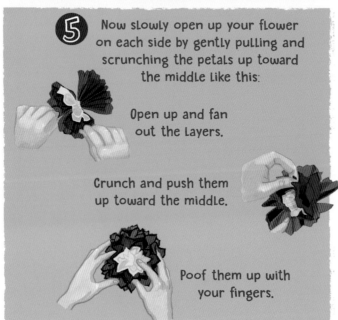

6 Keep pulling and scrunching the petals to shape your flower.

You've just made
FLORES DE NAVIDAD!
¡Excelente trabajo!

Published by Two Lions, New York www.apub.com · Amazon, the Amazon Logo, and Two Lions are trademarks of Amazon.com, Inc., or its affiliates.
ISBN-13: 9781542028004 (hardcover) · ISBN-10: 1542028000 (hardcover) The illustrations are rendered in digital media.
Book design by AndWorld Design Printed in China · First Edition · 10 9 8 7 6 5 4 3 2 1

Luces centelleantes

bastón de caramelo

bola de nieve

copos de nieve de papel

elfos deportistas

rana cascanueces

un jersey de Mamá

pudín de Navidad

piña brillante

Lazo para regalos

decoración increíble de Santa

almohadas navideñas

crackers de Navidad

Oh, Christmas Trees!

Believe in Mrs. Claus

cactus de Navidad

adorno de ángel para el árbol

muérdago

HO HO HO

add cookies!

by Kerry grade two